Ma... Good Idea

Story by Jenny Giles
Illustrations by Xiangyi Mo and Jingwen Wang

A Harcourt Achieve Imprint

www.Rigby.com
1-800-531-5015

James ran up
to the soccer ball
and tried to kick it
past his friend Matt.
"You won't stop
this one!" he shouted.

But Matt kicked
the ball away.

James ran to get it.
"Here it comes again!"
he called.

As he kicked
the soccer ball, he slipped.
The ball went flying up
into a tree.

"Oh!" cried Matt.
"It's not coming down!"

The ball was stuck
on a branch.

"Look at my soccer ball!"
said James.
"It's going to stay
up there.
What can we do?"

The boys looked up
at the branch.
"There is no way
we can get
that ball down,"
said James.

Matt ran
over to get his baseball.

Matt came back
to the tree
with the baseball.

"What are you going
to do with that?"
said James.

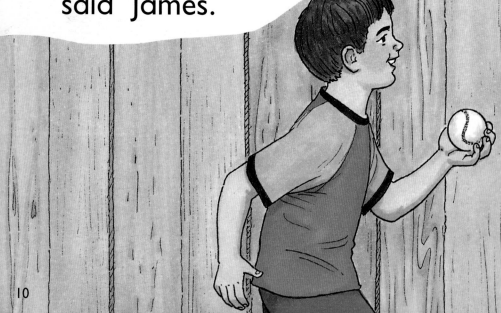

"I'm going to use it to get your soccer ball down from the tree," said Matt.
"Watch this!"

The baseball flew
up into the tree.
It hit the branch,
but the soccer ball
didn't move.

The baseball came down,
and Matt ran to get it.

"You won't get my soccer ball
down like that," said James.

"I'm going to try
one more time," said Matt.

The baseball flew
up again.

Thud!

This time it hit
the soccer ball.

"Good one, Matt!"
shouted James.

The boys cheered
as the two balls
fell to the ground.